A. J. Cosmo

ajcosmo.com

Nuts
(1st Print Edition)

Written by
A.J. Cosmo

Illustrated by
A.J. Cosmo

Edited by
Angela Pearson

Special Thanks to
Elizabeth Pursel

Production:
Thought Bubble Publishing

every family is a little

nuts

by a.j. cosmo

Wally looked out the car window as they drove.

"When do we get to open presents?" he asked.

"After dinner," said his mother, Brazil.

"Forty-eight," said Pistachio, Wally's little sister.

"What's that, sweetie?" asked Wally's father, Almond.

"She's counting dumb birds again," said Wally.

"Wally!" said Brazil.

"What?" replied Wally.

They arrived at Grandma's house and everyone got out.

"I want to see the birds," said Pistachio.

Her father bent down and patted her on the head.

"Alright but don't go too far and be back before dinner, okay?"

Pistachio nodded and skipped off to the forest.

Wally frowned.

"Give me a hand with the presents, Wally" said Brazil.

"Why isn't Pistachio helping?" Wally asked.

"Let Dad and I be the parents," Mom said, as she put a pile of presents in Wally's arms.

"Put those down and go see Grandma," said Almond.

"But all Grandma ever talks about is the time she found a coconut!" said Wally.

"You'd appreciate her if you talked to her more, now go," said Almond.

"But Dad..."

"No buts, go."

"Hello Grandma Praline," said Wally.

"Walnut! Look how you've grown," said Grandma.

"Yes, Grandma. It's been a whole year," said Wally.

"Has it now? Say, did I ever tell you about the time I found a coconut?"

"Only a million times, grandma."

"Well, what's the harm in hearing it again?"

A car pulled up and Wally jumped at the excuse.

"I better go see who that is," Wally said.

"Great to see you," Grandma said as he ran outside.

Outside, Wally's uncle, Peanut, was unloading a bunch of presents. Wally wondered if any were his.

"Wally! So good to see you! How are you doing? What's new? How's school going? Do you like your teachers? Do you have a girlfriend yet? What am I saying, girls are gross, right? Could you give me a hand with this?" Peanut said as he piled presents on Wally's arms.

"This is kind of heavy," Wally said, but it was no use, Peanut was already in the house. "Uncle Peanut?"

"He went inside," said Chestnut.

Wally turned around and almost screamed. Chestnut, his cousin, stared at him.

"Chestnut, you scared me," Wally said.

Chestnut stared.

"Um, how are you?" Wally asked.

"Fine," Chestnut said.

"Could you give me a hand with this?" Wally asked.

Chestnut slowly took a single present and went inside.

"Thanks, couldn't do it without you," Wally groaned.

"Wally? Is that you?" called Dad from the kitchen.
Wally put the presents down and looked for his name.
"Wally!"
"What?"
"Come help me in the kitchen!"
"I thought Mom was cooking," Wally said.
"She needed to draw something," Dad said.
"Why does she get to draw when we have to work?"
"Let her do her thing, Wally, now take these and go
set the table," Dad said as he handed Wally silverware.
Wally laid out the knives, forks, and spoons.

"Wally," Grandma called.

"What?" Wally yelled back.

"I want to tell you a story," grandma replied.

"Is it about a coconut?" Wally yelled.

"Yes!" Grandma said.

Wally finished setting the table and went to his dad.

"Can I go look at the presents now?" Wally asked.

"Okay, let's see how you did," Dad said as he checked the table. "Wally, forks go to the left of the plate."

"Why does that matter?" Wally asked.

"It's how it's done," Dad said as he corrected Wally's work. He was extra careful to line everything up.

"Why didn't you do it yourself then?" Wally asked.

"Because then you wouldn't have been helping me," Dad said as he went back to the kitchen.

Wally huffed, looked around, and moved a single fork back to the right side.

"Wally!" called Grandma.

"I'm busy, Grandma!" Wally yelled back.

Wally looked over the presents but couldn't find one with his name on it. Another car arrived and he ran outside to see who it was.

"Aunt Acorn!" Wally said.

Aunt Acorn smiled and went to hug her nephew, but he ducked past her and headed for the trunk.

"Do you need help carrying presents?" Wally asked.

"Oh that's so sweet of you. Here, take this little one, I can get the rest," Acorn said as she loaded up.

"I can carry more, Aunt Acorn," Wally said.

"Oh it's no trouble at all," Acorn said as she struggled to carry everything.

Wally looked to make sure no presents were left in the car and noticed that his cousin Cashew was in the backseat on her phone.

"Hello, Cashew," Wally said.
Cashew rolled her eyes and got out of the car...

"Good to see you, too," Wally said.

Wally put down the present and looked for his name
again. Acorn had rearranged everything though, and
Wally had to start looking all over again.

"Wally!" called Grandma.

"Yes Grandma Praline," Wally yelled.

"Come here, I want to tell you a story!"

"Can't Grandma, Mom needs my help," Wally yelled.

Wally made his way through the crowded kitchen. Acorn
was busy making thirty or so side dishes while Dad
kept an eye on the oven and Peanut tried to help.

"Where's Mom?" Wally asked.

"She's in the garage," Almond said. "Don't bother her."

Wally nodded and went straight for the garage.

"Moooommmm," Wally said.

Brazil looked up from her drawing and squinted.

"Yes?" she said.

"What are you drawing?" Wally asked.

"Remember that gourd painting I was hired to do?
I think I finally fixed it. I'm not sure. What do you
think?" Brazil asked as she showed him the drawing.
Wally looked at it but didn't know what to say.

"You're right. It's awful." Brazil said.

"No," Wally said. "I... I was just looking at it."

"Well, what do you think? Tell me, I can take it."

"It looks good, Mom, like a gourd," Wally said.

Mom shook her head.

"What's wrong?" Wally asked.

"You're right, it's not working," she said as she tore up the picture.

"Mom!" Wally cried.

"I can do better. Thank you, Wally," she said.

"Okay..." Wally said as he left.

He felt bad and didn't know why.

Wally walked into a kitchen full of smoke.

He coughed. "What's going on?"

Acorn opened the windows and waved the smoke outside.

Peanut laughed as he coughed.

"What happened?" Wally asked.

"Your pops burned the roast," Peanut said.

"It's all my fault, Acorn said. "I needed help finding the salt and we lost track of time."

"What are we going to eat now?" Wally asked.

Dad put the roast on the counter and took off his oven mitts. "You worry too much, Wally."

"I seem to be the only one who does!"

Cashew laughed.

"What's so funny?" Wally barked.

Cashew rolled her eyes and went back to her phone.

"I'll cut off the burned parts. It will be fine," Almond said. "Now do me a favor and go get your sister."

"She should have been back by now," Wally said.

"You either get her or you go listen to Grandma."

Wally groaned and went outside.

"Pistachio!" Wally called. "Dinner time! Pistachio!"
Wally walked into the woods to find his sister.
"There you are! You'd get in trouble if they knew you
were out this far," Wally said.
Pistachio didn't move. She was just staring at the sky.
"Come on, it's dinnertime," Wally said as he took her
hand and pulled. She pulled right back.
"Ouch," Wally said. "Watch it!"
Pistachio didn't look at him- she just stared up.
"Aren't you hungry?" Wally asked.
Pistachio didn't speak.
"Aren't you bored?" Wally teased.

Pistachio squeezed his hand and pointed. Just like that, a swan appeared and flew by. Wally was amazed. The bird was huge and white and seemed like it shouldn't fly, but yet it did- and it was amazing.

The bird flew off and Pistachio let go of his hand. Wally didn't move though, his heart was pounding. After a moment he quietly said "Come on."

Wally and Pistachio got to the dinner table as Dad put the final touches on the silverware.

"I'm so sorry," Acorn said. "I would have sworn forks go on the right."

"If you really want to mess with him you hide the spoons!" Peanut laughed.

"It's fine," Dad said. "Thanks for getting your sister, Wally. Did you see any birds, Pistachio?"

"I saw five. That makes fifty-three," Pistachio said.

"That's wonderful sweetie," Almond replied. "Go wash your hands, we're about to eat."

Pistachio went to the bathroom and Wally sat down.

"Presents after this?" Wally asked.

"You already knew that," Dad said.

Mom came in and sat next to Wally.

"That drawing was hard," she said. "Wally gave me some tough love but he was right."

"What did you say to her, Wally?" Dad asked.

"I have no idea," Wally replied.

"Who's hungry? I'm hungry," Peanut said.

"Goodness me, we forgot Mom!" Acorn said. She came back a few moments later with her arm around Praline. "Don't mind this old thing," Praline said as she sat down. "I know why you're all here."

"Food and presents," Chestnut said.

Grandma Praline laughed. "That's right."

"Can we eat?" Cashew said while looking at her phone.

"Oh, Cashew," Acorn laughed. "I keep telling her she should be a comedian."

Brazil led everyone in prayer and they all sat down. Before the food even made it around the table, Peanut took his plate and went to the living room.

He turned on the TV and ate alone.

"Why does Uncle Peanut get to watch TV?" Wally asked.

"It's his thing," Mom said.

"Can I watch TV, too?" Wally asked.

"When you have a mortgage, Wally," Dad said.
Wally slumped down but smiled when he saw the
spaghetti squash heading towards him.
Chestnut took the rest of the spaghetti squash and
dumped it on his plate.
"Hey!" Wally cried.
Chestnut stared back at Wally.
"I wanted some of that!" Wally said.
"Did he eat all the squash?" Peanut called from the
living room. "Sorry about that, it's all he eats. I
usually make extra."

"There's plenty of other things to eat, Wally," Brazil said as she offered him some corn.

Wally growled and took the corn.

"But I didn't want corn," Wally mumbled.

"Would you all like to hear about the time I found a coconut?" Grandma asked.

"No, Grandma," everyone said.

Dinner was delicious and Wally rushed to clean up.

"You're so helpful," Acorn said as Wally brought her the dishes.

"I'm proud of you," said Dad as Wally took out the trash.

"Just doing my job," Wally said. "Anything else?"

"I think that just about covers it," Brazil said.

"Yes!" Wally said and he rushed to the living room.

He may not have known which present was his, but he knew somewhere in that pile there was one for him.

Chestnut stood in front of the presents.

Wally couldn't understand what was wrong with him.

"Chestnut?" Wally asked. "What's up with you?"

Wally snapped his fingers right in Chestnut's ears.

Chestnut covered his ears and screamed.

"Loud!" cried Chestnut.

Wally backed off.

"What happened?" Peanut asked as he ran over.

"I was just trying to get his attention," Wally said.

"All I did was snap my fingers near his ears.

Why is he freaking out?"

"He hears really well, Wally," Peanut said.

"I don't understand," Wally said.

Peanut took his son and hugged him.

"It's okay, Chestnut," Peanut said as he hummed.
Chestnut calmed down.
"Is he going to be alright?" Wally asked.
"He just got scared, that's all," Peanut said.
"I didn't mean to," Wally said.
Peanut smiled. "It's fine, Wally, seriously."

The time for presents came and the whole family gathered around to open them. Peanut announced the name and Cashew delivered the gift. Mom got a new paint set while Dad got a new vacuum cleaner. Cashew got a gift card. Peanut received a remote control. Acorn opened an electric blanket. Grandma was delighted with her back pillow and Pistachio loved her binoculars. But as the last present was opened, Wally's heart broke.

"Is that all of them?" Wally asked.

"Unless I missed one. Nope. That's all of them."

"Are you sure?" Wally asked again.

"I'm sure it's here somewhere," Brazil said.

"We didn't forget you, Wally," Dad said.

"There are no presents left," Chestnut said plainly.

Cashew looked up from her phone and seemed to care.

Wally sniffled, rubbed his eyes, and told himself not to cry, but after a crazy day he had had enough, and the tears flowed.

"It's not fair!" Wally shouted.

He ran outside and slammed the door behind him.

Daddy Almond stood to go but Grandma cleared her throat and stopped him.

"I'll deal with this," Praline said.

Praline took her cane and walked to the back of the house. Behind the shed, next to the garbage, was Wally curled up in a ball, crying.

Grandma Praline took a seat next to him and waited for him to say something.

"Everyone hates me," Wally finally said.

"Is that so?" Grandma asked.

"Nobody loves me," Wally sobbed.

"Really now? No one?" grandma said.

"Yes! Everyone is crazy but me!" Wally said.

Grandma Praline laughed. "Even me?" she asked.

Wally sniffled and didn't say anything.

"That's a yes then," Grandma said. "Oh Wally, Wally,
Wally, Wally... What do you feel inside right now?"
"I don't know."
"Yes you do. What are you feeling?"
Wally wiped his nose and felt his heart.
"Mad," he said.
"And what's under that feeling?"
"I don't know."
"You do, sweetheart. Just look at what's under mad."
Wally felt some more. "Sad," he said.
"And below that?"
Wally dried his eyes.

"It feels like, like nobody wants me," Wally said.

Grandma nodded. "Does that sound like the truth?"

"No," he said, "but everyone is crazy."

Granma Praline laughed. "We're all a little crazy, sweetheart, that's what makes us normal. Do you think I've ever judged you?"

"Me?" Wally asked. "What's wrong with me?"

Grandma smiled. "Oh everything has a label, dear. Everyone loses their marbles once in a while."

"Is there something wrong with me?" Wally asked.

Grandma shrugged. "I don't think so. Then again, I'm not as smart as an eight year old."

"Do they hate me, Grandma?" Wally asked.

"They love you, Wally. I know it can be hard to tell the difference sometimes."

Wally laughed and curled up against her.

"Let them be just as they are, Okay? I promise they'll do the same for you," Praline said.

"Thank you Grandma," he said.

She smiled and rubbed his back.

"Did I ever tell you about the time I found a coconut?" Wally smiled. "No Grandma, tell me."

By the time Wally and Praline came inside, the whole house was clean and everyone was enjoying desert. "All better," Praline said as she nudged Wally. "Would you like some hot cocoa?" Dad asked. Wally nodded. "We figured out what happened," Mom said. "It's all my fault," Acorn said. "I had your name but I must have left the present while packing for Cashew. I'm so, so sorry, I'll ship it to you the moment I get back. I promise I'll make it up to you." "It's okay," Wally said. "Accidents happen." "I'll make it up to you," Acorn said.

"I know you didn't mean to forget it," Wally said.

Dad returned with hot cocoa for Wally.

"Extra marshmallows," he said.

"Just like I like it," Wally smiled.

"I made you this with Mom's supplies," Pistachio said.

She handed Wally a beautiful and very detailed drawing of a Swan.

"I hope you like it."

Wally was amazed. The drawing was perfect.

"It's beautiful," Wally said.
"It's your swan," she said.
"It's our swan," Wally said.
Pistachio smiled.

Everyone said their goodbyes, packed up their presents, and got in their cars. The holiday was over and it was time to go home.

Grandma waved as they pulled away.

Wally waved back.

"We're coming back soon, right?" he asked.

"Yes, Wally," Mom smiled.

"Before you know it," Dad said.

"Fifty-four," Pistachio said.

"Fifty-four," Wally smiled.

The end.

for my family &

Andro & Marissa

Hunter & Missyface

Katie & Jimmy Luff

Kenny & Anthony

Travis Friend

Kerri K.
(mother of Zachary,
Rebecca, & Jean-Paul)

Camdyn & Aubrey's
grandma

Bobbi Capwell

Jack Nesta Tripp

Meeblette

Jarod, Ayrianna &
James

Skyler & Sophia

Donna Harvey

Victoria Jacobsmeyer

MeMaw, Vicky, &
Sophia Smith

Kari B.

Kirsten L.

Caydon & Avery
Cowell

thought bubble
PUBLISHING

Made in the USA
Lexington, KY
09 December 2017